W9-BLQ-057

Little Patriot Press

WOODROW
FOR
PRESIDENT

A Tail of Voting, Campaigns, and Elections

By **Peter W. Barnes** and **Cheryl Shaw Barnes**

Cataloging-in-Publication data on file with the Library of Congress
ISBN 978-1-59698-786-9

Published in the United States by
Regnery Publishing, Inc.
One Massachusetts Avenue, NW
Washington, DC 20001
www.Regnery.com

Manufactured in the United States of America
10 9 8 7 6 5 4 3 2 1

Books are available in quantity for promotional or premium use. For information
on discounts and terms write to Director of Special Sales, Regnery Publishing, Inc.,
One Massachusetts Avenue, NW, Washington, DC, 2001, or call 202-216-0600.

Distributed to the trade by:
Perseus Distribution
387 Park Avenue South
New York, NY 10016

This book is dedicated to

the men and women
of the United States Secret Service,
for their hard work on behalf of candidates,
presidents, and their families.

—P.W.B. and C.S.B.

Find the mouse Secret Service agent
hidden in each illustration.

When Woodrow G. Washingtail was just a baby,
His mother and father said, "Someday, just maybe,
He'll grow up to be, with great celebration,
The president of the entire mouse nation!"

His parents made sure that he grew tall and strong,
That he valued hard work, that he knew right from wrong,
That he ate all his spinach and he ate all his peas,
That he ate all his mouse macaroni and cheese.

He worked hard in school and—all students note—
At 18 years old, he registered to vote!
He graduated college the first in his class—
"Mousa Cum Laude" and a medal of brass.

Then Woodrow, all-American mouse of renown
Went back to Moussouri, back to his hometown
To open a shop, marry Bess, his good wife.
They started a family and a wonderful life!

But here's where his story is just getting started...
For Woodrow, they say, was extremely big-hearted:
He'd close up his store at the end of each day,
Go home, where he and the children would play,

Help Bess with the supper, then like a good dad,
Help the kids finish all of the homework they had.
But this isn't where his big-heartedness ends—
He also helped other mice—neighbors and friends.

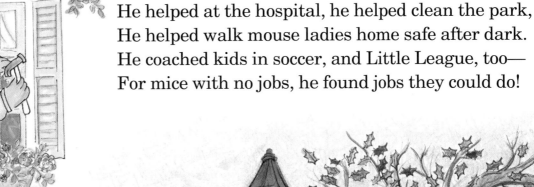

He helped at the hospital, he helped clean the park,
He helped walk mouse ladies home safe after dark.
He coached kids in soccer, and Little League, too—
For mice with no jobs, he found jobs they could do!

MOUSSOURI
COTTAGE
HOSPITAL

For you see, Woodrow knew he'd been blessed from the start—
Given such a good life, that he felt in his heart
That someone like him should *give back*, with good grace—
To help make his town—and the world—a good place.

One day, Woodrow's friends said, "Woodrow, we hear
There's a seat on town council that is open this year.
With your heart and your brains, we agree you'd be great,
If you ran for the job, as our mouse candidate!"

A "candidate," in our nation's tradition,
Is someone who seeks an important position
By entering a contest called an "election,"
And citizens "vote" to make their selection.

You vote For or Against to express your own view
Of a candidate (or issue) important to you,
In private, in secret, without fear or fright—
In our democracy, it's our most basic right.

But more on this later, for Woodrow, you see,
Was elected to council—unani-mouse-ly!
He did such good work—with skill and with care,
The next thing you know, they elected him mayor!

They elected him later (it seems like a blur)
To the state capital as a state senator!
He served the mice well—they just couldn't wait—
They elected him *governor* of the *whole state*!

When Governor Woodrow, now older and wise,
Finished his term (this should be no surprise),
Bess and his friends said, "All the time you have spent
Helping others would make you a great president!"

Woodrow, so humbled, replied, "If you please—
Are you sure I could serve as the nation's 'Big Cheese?'"
"We are certain!" they shouted. "So now don't delay!"
He declared himself *candidate* the very next day!

WOODROW G WASHINGTAIL FOR PRESIDENT

WE WANT WOODROW

BULL MOUSE PARTY WOODROW

A "MICE" CHOICE FOR PRESIDENT

So many elections—state, local, and more—
So many good candidates—they run by the score.
But running for president is different, we'll show,
For it's such an important position, you know.

First, every candidate must, to explain,
Hire assistants and form a "campaign."
But a presidential candidate often creates
A *big, big* campaign, for all 50 states!

A candidate needs "volunteers" by the dozens—
Friends, neighbors, supporters, aunts, uncles, and cousins!
Volunteers help for free—for no compensation—
When their candidate, they feel, will be good for the nation.

A campaign needs offices, computers, and flags,
Buttons and posters and banners and bags!
Volunteers and assistants—there's so much to do!
(If you like a candidate, you can volunteer, too!)

INDEPENDENT

DEMOCRATS

GREENBACK LABOR

LIBERTY

AMERICAN PARTY

STATES RIGHTS DEMOCRATIC PARTY

FREE SOIL

SINGLE TAX

PEOPLES PARTY

FEDERALIST

PROGRESSIVE PARTY

GREEN

LAND REFORM

VEGETARIAN PARTY

©1912 PROGRESSIVE

A "political party" is part of campaigning—
A phrase, we agree, that needs some explaining:
We don't mean a party with candles or cake
Or presents for birthdays—don't make that mistake.

A *political* party and its "politicians"
Is one group of citizens with common positions—
They all work together on ideas they share
About how our nation should work and prepare.

For instance, one party's ideas may include
Helping farmers to increase production of food.
There might be a party that favors a rule
That doubles the number of classes at school!

There may be a party that might find it dandy
If neighborhood stores would stop selling candy!
So many positions and so many views—
So many good parties to study or choose!

Political parties have existed, you see,
From the start of America's long history:
Democrat, Republican, Libertarian, Green,
Reform and Progressive are a few we have seen.

Someday when you're older, you may well decide
To join a political party with pride.
To which party does our friend Woodrow belong?
The "Bull Mouse," of course, so upright and strong.

Not so fast, Mister Woodrow, for you're not alone—
Other mice in your party have let it be known:
Each says he or she could be president, too.
So what happens next? What's a party to do?

In this case, when two mice or four mice or eight,
Each believes he or she is the best candidate,
A party needs some way to make a selection—
One way is to hold a "primary" election.

Party members decide for themselves in each state
If they want to establish a primary date.
If they do, they invite the contestants competing
To visit their state, for speaking and meeting.

The state of Mouse Hampshire, a wonderful place,
Is home to the very first primary race.
It's also where candidates meet to debate
The serious issues that carry great weight.

At one debate, Woodrow jumped in the first minute,
Though Senator Trumouse was sure he would win it.
Another good governor, Greytail, spoke true,
So did Senator Fieldmouse, and Ed Mouse-ski, too!

But Woodrow was better, debating with ease—
He talked about jobs, the production of cheese,
About helping poor church mice—and then, very soon—
About sending astronaut mice to the moon!

ELECT WOODROW

Woodrow won in Mouse Hampshire, the start of his quest,
Then won other primaries, north, south, east, and west,
By working long hours and traveling for weeks
For debates, shaking paws, kissing mouse babies' cheeks!

The victories showed clearly—reporters agreed—
Governor Woodrow had taken the lead
To be, for his party, its great "nominee"
For the land's highest office, the presidency!

WOODROW PRESIDENT

WE WANT WOODROW

WOODROW

WOODROW

After the primaries, party members are sent
In state "delegations" to one big event—
A *national convention*, a meeting so glorious,
To formally nominate Woodrow, victorious!

The delegates travel by train and by car
They travel in airplanes and buses, so far.
Party delegates come with a duty, it's noted—
Representing all members and how they have voted.

The convention begins, every delegate waits
For the famous, historic "Roll Call of the States."
The delegates whoop and they jump and they cheer
With each state's decree, one by one, that they hear.

"The great state of Moussouri," its delegates shout,
"Casts its votes for the mouse that, without any doubt,
Will be our next president—we know he can't fail—
Its favorite son, WOODROW G. WASHINGTAIL!!!!"

And on down the list, every state makes its choice,
Until all the delegates can say with one voice
To mice everywhere, a great declaration:
Woodrow has won the Bull Mouse nomination!

"Woodrow! Woodrow!" they chant and they call
To the top of the roof, to the top of the hall.
He steps to the podium, the new nominee,
To announce, "My dear friends, I accept—gratefully!"

MOUSSOURI

MOUSSISSIPPI

A BULL MOUSE FOR THE WHITE HOUSE

EVERYBODY WINS WITH WOODROW

RODENT RIGHTS

WOODROW

AMERICA LOVES WOODROW

W.W.

BULL MOUSE

WIN WITH WOODROW

WOODROW

The nominee now has a very big task—
He must decide quickly which mouse he will ask
To be his vice president—number two "on the slate"—
The very best partner, the best "running mate."

Woodrow, his assistants, and party leaders agreed
One mouse from the primaries could surely succeed
As Woodrow's vice president—clearly, all knew it:
Senator Felicity Fieldmouse could do it!

The convention went wild! And by acclamation,
Every mouse on the floor, every state delegation
Voted that choice (they knew how to pick it)—
Senator Fieldmouse was now "on the ticket."

A president is elected, we hope you remember,
Every four years in the month of November.
In "general" elections, with primaries completed,
Campaigning begins once again—it's repeated.

So off for more picnics the candidates go,
More speeches and meetings, in rain, sleet, or snow.
On the "campaign trail" is no time to shirk—
For being a candidate is very hard work!

That's because Woodrow, despite his great fame,
Was not the only big mouse in the game—
The Country Mouse Party had held its convention,
And its nominee was now in contention:

Senator Rufus C. Tuftmouse (retired)
Was widely respected and widely admired.
One of his bills (it passed Congress with ease)
Created the U.S. Department of Cheese!

Tuftmouse and his campaign hit the trail,
Battling Woodrow toe-to-toe, tail-to-tail!
To help voters choose the best candidate,
They agreed to a nationwide TV debate!

The voters tuned in to listen and learn,
Each mouse debating the issues in turn,
Discussing their plans and their hopes and their fears—
The viewers, reporters, the rest were all ears!

When it was over, the cheers and applause
Filled the room as the candidates met and shook paws.
"America's voters," Woodrow thought, "hold my fate.
So all I can do now is sit back and wait."

Election Day came, and most mice, with delight,
Exercised their basic, constitutional right,
To go the "polls," to each cast one vote.
(Our democracy working, historians note.)

Voters cast votes different ways, we have seen,
Some mark paper "ballots," some vote by machine.
Whatever the method, every vote counts
When election officials add up the amounts.

After they voted back home in Moussouri,
Woodrow and Bess, with the kids, in a hurry,
Rushed to a downtown hotel to await
As voting results were announced for each state.

The polls closed. Hours passed. And then, suddenly,
Senator Tuftmouse appeared on TV!
"The voters have spoken," Tuftmouse conceded—
The vote total showed he had been defeated!

"Woodrow has won," Rufus said with respect.
"Let's all now support him—our *president-elect*!"
In a ballroom downstairs, Woodrow walked into cheers
From friends and supporters and great volunteers!

"Dear friends, I am honored," Woodrow began,
"You've elected me president of this great land.
A difficult job—I'll be put to the test.
But I promise to work hard and give you my best!"

On January 20th, Inauguration Day,
Woodrow stood before all, to swear and to say
He'd uphold and protect our great Constitution
And each citizen's rights, with firm resolution.

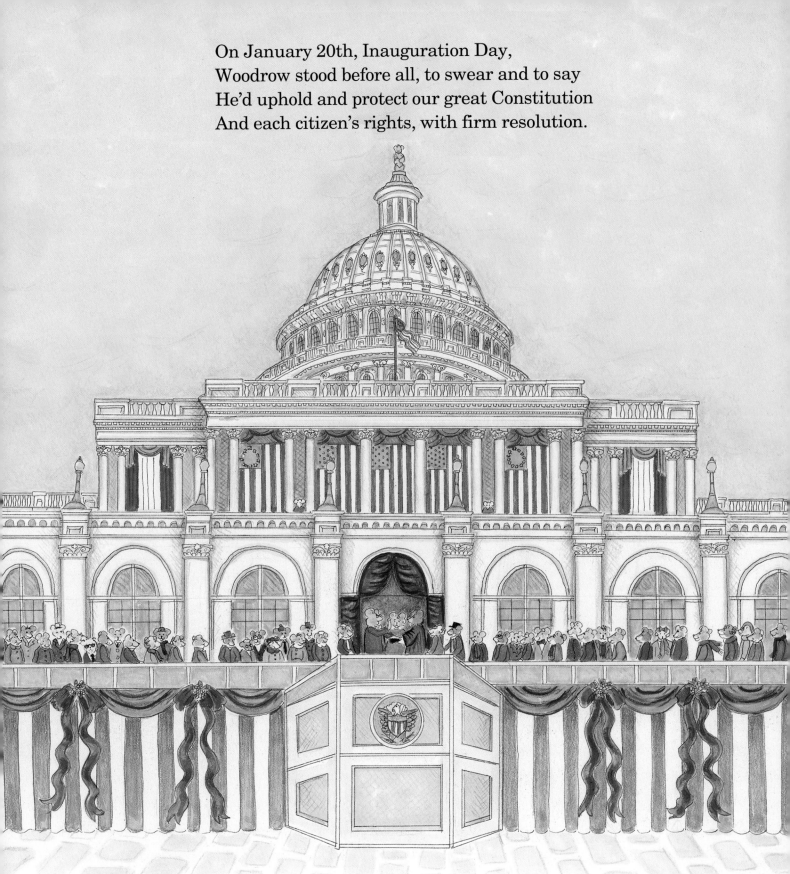

Once sworn in, he began his "Inaugural Address"—
A speech to the nation, a way to express
His plans and his dreams for all mice to share.
And then he declared to mice everywhere:

"Ask *not* what your nation can do for you," he said,
"Ask what *you* can do for your nation, instead—
And for your community and neighbors, so close,
For your friends and your family—that's what matters most!

"Vote! Get involved! Volunteer! That's what's right—
Be a good citizen—be your own *point of light*!"
The crowd cheered "Hooray!" for this wonderful mouse
As he walked down the street to the famous White House—

Where Woodrow and Bess and their girls and the boys,
Arrived with their suitcases, boxes, and toys
To begin Woodrow's term, his "administration,"
The hope of all mice, the hope of a nation.

That night, Bess and Woodrow danced down the Great Hall,
Honored hosts of the splendid Inaugural Ball.
With friends and supporters, they hob and they nob,
The night before Woodrow begins his new job.

After the ball, the new president said,
"Enough celebration—it's now time for bed,
For tomorrow, I have, when I wake from my sleep,
Many dreams to fulfill, many promises to keep."

The Tail End
Resources for Parents and Teachers

Growing Up to Be President

Do you want to grow up to be president? The Constitution says that to become president, you have to be at least 35 years old and a "natural born" U.S. citizen, which generally means born in a state or U.S. territory. You also must have lived in the U.S. for at least 14 years.

The youngest president was Theodore Roosevelt, who was 42 when he became president in 1901. The oldest was Ronald Reagan. He was 69 when he was elected in 1980.

Most presidents serve in public office before they get to the White House. President Reagan was governor of California. President John F. Kennedy was a senator and a congressman. Some were military leaders. Our first president, George Washington, was commander of the Continental Army during the Revolutionary War.

Helping Your Community

If you like to go to the park, read books, or clean up, you can help your community! Most people do this by volunteering. You can join groups that pick up trash in parks or teach reading. People can volunteer at schools, hospitals, or places of worship. If they can't give their time, they can donate food, clothes, or money to help those in need. Sometimes being involved in your community is as simple as being a good friend or neighbor. Whatever you do, the experience can teach you about being a better person and important life lessons. Many times, helping this way—"giving back"—makes you feel good, too!

Another way to help others is by working in government. We call people who do this "public servants." The president is a public servant; so are the mayor of your town, the commissioner of your county, and the governor of your state. Citizens who serve in the military are, too. A lot of people in government, such as members of your local school board or city council, work for free, without pay, because they think it is important and will make their community better.

The Tail End
Resources for Parents and Teachers

Running for President

President Theodore Roosevelt liked to box. In President Roosevelt's time, when a person wanted to challenge someone to box, he tossed his hat into the boxing ring.

So when Roosevelt announced in 1912 that he planned to run for president again, he told voters, "My hat's in the ring." But it is not enough to simply throw your hat in the ring. A candidate needs to get his or her name put on each state's ballot. Most states require candidates to collect lots of signatures on petitions. This can be a lot of work, so serious candidates often ask volunteers to help gather them.

Political Campaigns

"I Like Ike!" That's what a group of ordinary citizens said when they asked retired General Dwight D. Eisenhower, whose nickname was Ike, to run for president in 1952. They got together and worked hard to get him elected. That is basically all a campaign is—a group of people working together on behalf of a candidate or an issue.

A presidential campaign can be tough. Candidates travel far and wide, visiting many states for months, sometimes years. They meet people and tell them their ideas and goals—their "campaign promises." The candidate explains why he or she would make the best leader. Volunteers in a campaign send letters, organize events, hand out buttons and flyers, and do everything they can to get the word out about their candidate and get them votes! "I Like Ike" buttons were very popular in the 1952 election!

The Tail End
Resources for Parents and Teachers

Political Parties

Do you think everyone should eat only vegetables? If so, then you might have joined the Vegetarian Party! Like campaigns, political parties are made up of groups of committed people. They share a set of common beliefs and set up an organization to support and promote them. They also help select leaders to run for office. That is what happened in 1947, when a group of people thought that the only food we should eat were vegetables.

Voters have formed dozens of parties throughout the nation's history. They include the "Silver" Party, the "Bull Moose" Party, the "Greenback" Party, and the "Tea" Party. The Democratic and Republican parties are the dominant parties today.

Primaries and Caucuses

There are really two parts to a presidential election—the parties' nominating process and the general election. In the first part, political parties organize "primary" elections in many states to help their members choose one candidate from any who "throw their hat in the ring." The candidates from the same party travel to different states to compete with each other by talking to voters and debating. Then on a certain day, party members go to voting places—polls—to choose one candidate to be their "nominee," one person to represent the party in the general election in November.

In a few states, party members choose their top candidate in meetings called "caucuses." Regardless of the method, party members select delegates to represent their choice at the party's main meeting, its convention.

The Constitution allows a president to serve only two consecutive four-year terms. Generally, an incumbent president who wants to run for re-election is automatically his party's nominee and gets to skip this process the second time around.

The Tail End
Resources for Parents and Teachers

Political Conventions

Political conventions are an exciting end to the nominating process—big celebrations with lots of colorful banners, buttons, signs, and flags that last several days. At the meeting, delegates formally approve their nominee, who is usually the person who got the most votes in the primaries and caucuses. Delegates vote, one state at a time, in the "roll call of the states." Once a candidate gets the majority of votes, he or she is declared the winner.

After this, the delegates vote on the person who will be the vice presidential candidate, the nominee's "running mate." The presidential and vice presidential candidates together are referred to as the party's "ticket."

Campaign Trail

After the convention, the nominees quickly hit the "campaign trail" again, this time for the general election. Once again, the candidates travel all around the country. They meet more voters. They answer more questions about the important issues. They might travel to several states in one day!

The nominees from each party debate each other before the entire nation. They present their positions and question each other's goals and ideas. Candidates may criticize each other during debates, but at the beginning and the end, they shake hands and hope that there are no hard feelings.

Election Day

Under federal law, every four years, the first Tuesday after the first Monday in November is Election Day for the presidency as well as other offices. The polling places, usually in public buildings like schools, are run by volunteers who make sure each person gets to vote, fairly and in private.

In America's early years, generally only white men who owned land could vote. Over time, however, the nation expanded the right to vote to include more citizens. Now nearly all American adults—men and women of every race over the age of 18 who are citizens—can vote.

The Tail End
Resources for Parents and Teachers

Declaring a Winner

After the polls close on Election Day, state officials collect and report votes. Usually the candidate who wins the majority of votes is the winner. But under the Constitution, when people cast their votes, they are actually voting for "electors" who make the final selection in a national "Electoral College." Each state has a certain number of electoral votes based on its population—the more people, the more votes. There are 538 total electoral votes.

In most states, the winner of the popular vote gets all the electoral votes. Throughout election night, people follow news reports as states go to one candidate or another. Once one of them accumulates 270 electoral votes, a simple majority, that candidate is the next president.

Inauguration Day

January 20th in the year after the election is Inauguration Day. The president and vice president are sworn in at the U.S. Capitol in a big ceremony. The new president makes a speech to the nation, an Inaugural Address. After the ceremony, the president joins a parade to the White House. The day ends with many states and organizations hosting Inaugural Balls—and lots of dancing!

Additional Information and Activities

Woodrow for President stresses the importance of civic and community involvement in good citizenship. This includes volunteering, registering to vote, and participating in the political process by voting and other activities. One of the ways citizens can become active in the process is by running for elected office—local, state, or federal.

The U.S. Constitution and several constitutional amendments created the framework for electing a president and the voting rights of citizens. Article II, Clause I, of the Constitution declares that a president will serve a term of four years. The Constitution does not specify a date for election days for the presidency. Rather, the date of the first Tuesday after the first Monday in November was established by Congress itself, through federal statute. Voting rights were established in various clauses in, and amendments to, the Constitution. But the practice of direct election of officeholders by individual citizens, rather than state legislators or elite gentry, was mandated first in the Constitution for the House of Representatives, in Article I, Section II, Clause I, which declares members will be chosen "by the People of the several states." Eligibility requirements for voting (age, property holdings, etc.) were initially determined by each state individually. Several amendments to the Constitution expanded voting rights for women, minorities, and people 18 to 20 years old.

The Constitution makes no mention of political parties, campaigns, primaries, or conventions. The tradition of political parties, however, is rooted in the British political system, with its conservative Tories and liberal Whigs of the 1600s. The Founding Fathers and other early political leaders quickly organized their own parties after the states ratified the Constitution. There have been many dominant parties throughout the nation's history; the Democratic and Republican are the major parties today. Early on, the parties developed procedures for selecting candidates for the presidency and other major public offices. The two most popular methods today are state primaries and caucuses (party meetings). *Woodrow for President* focuses on the primary process, which is the principal method of the political parties for choosing presidential candidates today.

Contract to Vote

On the following page, children and adults can apply the lessons of
Woodrow for President by completing the "Contract to Vote Between
America's Children and Adults." Read and discuss the terms of the
contract together and then sign it. Post a copy of the contract in a central
location, such as on a refrigerator door, to remind all parties of the terms.

Contract to Vote
Between America's Children and Adults

This agreement, dated _____, is between

_____
(print name/names of child/children)

and

_____
(print name/names of adult/adults)

The parties acknowledge and agree that participation and involvement in the affairs of our community, state and nation are necessary for responsible citizenship and to the functioning of a free democracy. The parties also agree that the adult or adults named herein acknowledge that voting in local, state and national elections is the minimum requirement for responsible citizenship under the U.S. Constitution and the duty of all Americans of voting age. Therefore, the parties herein agree to the following terms and conditions:

1. The adults named herein acknowledge that it is their right, duty and responsibility as citizens of the United States of America to vote in all local, state and national elections, and that said adults pledge, promise and affirm to the children named herein that, as the future health, strength and safety of democracy depends on the adults' participation in the American political process, they will vote in all said elections from this date, forward. If the adults named herein are not yet registered to vote, they agree to register promptly.

2. The adults named herein pledge, promise and affirm that, as the future health, strength and safety of American democracy depends on the active involvement and participation of the children of the next generation in the political process, they will take, escort and direct any child named herein to their local polling places on all election days cited in Paragraph 1, to teach them and set an example for good citizenship.

3. For their part, the children named herein pledge, promise and affirm to identify, record and note in their own personal records the date of any and every election day in the current calendar year, and to notify the adults named herein in person or in writing one week before said dates, and then again one day before said dates, and then again the morning of said dates, so that the adults party to this agreement shall have no reason or excuse NOT to know the dates, and to remind, urge, coax, exhort, bug, nudge, needle, beseech, entreat, request, demand, goad, implore, induce, incite, beg, bribe, push, ply, or force and to otherwise use any and all means necessary to ensure that the said adults arrive at their neighborhood polling place on election days and exercise their constitutional right, duty and responsibility to vote.

4. The children named herein pledge, promise and affirm to register to vote upon turning the age of 18 years old and to exercise their constitutional duty and obligation to vote in all local, state and federal elections from that year, forward.

In other words, we all promise each other we will participate in the American political process and VOTE (adults now, children when they turn 18 years old), because it's so important to the future of our nation.

_____
(child/children's signatures)

_____
(adult/adults' signatures)

Acknowledgements

We wish to acknowledge the help, support,
and assistance of our friend Betty Shepard,
a retired elementary school librarian and teacher,
in the production of this book and supporting materials.
A special thanks to Eleanor Reed for her brilliant
writing and editing expertise. We also thank
our friends at the League of Women Voters,
Cheryl Graeve and Monica Sullivan,
for their editorial suggestions.

—P.W.B. and C.S.B.